D1556237

E   Hoban, Russell
HOB   Arthur's new power

DATE			
CARY	MAY 8	Jen	
parent	OCT 29 '80	OCT 18 '85	
NOV 7 '79	DEC 10 '80	APR 11 '86	
	SEP 25 '81	OCT 31 '86	
NOV 14 '79			
NOV 21 '79	Devault		
21. 9	FEB 26 '82	NOV 14 '86	
DEC 12 '79	MAR 5 '88	JAN 23 '87	
DEC 19 '79	MAR 26 '82	MAR 6 '87	
FEB 20 '80	franti	FEB 1 9 '88	
MAR 19	NOV 18 '83	CB 18	
MAY	Porter	APR 01	
	JAN 16 '85		

© THE BAKER & TAYLOR CO.

Arthur's New Power

by Russell Hoban
pictures by Byron Barton

Thomas Y. Crowell   New York

DAVIS JOINT UNIFIED SCHOOLS
NORTH DAVIS ELEMENTARY

Text copyright © 1978 by Russell Hoban
Illustrations copyright © 1978 by Byron Barton
All rights reserved. Printed in the United States of America. No part of this book may
be used or reproduced in any manner whatsoever without written permission except in the
case of brief quotations embodied in critical articles and reviews. For information address
Thomas Y. Crowell, 10 East 53 Street, New York, N. Y. 10022.
Published simultaneously in Canada by Fitzhenry & Whiteside Limited, Toronto.
First Edition

Library of Congress Cataloging in Publication Data
Hoban, Russell. Arthur's new power.
SUMMARY: A crocodile family tries to conserve energy at home.
[1. Energy conservation—Fiction. 2. Crocodiles—Fiction]
I. Barton, Byron. II. Title
PZ7.H637Ar   [E]   77-11550
ISBN 0-690-01370-1 ISBN 0-690-01371-X lib. bdg.
1 2 3 4 5 6 7 8 9 10

One evening Father Crocodile came
home and all the other houses on the road
were lit but his was dark.

Father went into the kitchen.
Mother Crocodile was doing yoga
and their daughter Emma was doing
homework by the light of a candle.
"What happened this time?" said Father.

"Arthur again," said Emma. "He plugged
in his new Dracula Hi-Vamp
and everything went black."

"What's that horrible noise?" said Father.

"Suction," said Emma,
"by The Plumber's Helpers."

"Did the drain back up or what?"
said Father.

"*Suction* is a new album by a group called
The Plumber's Helpers," said Emma.

Father went into Arthur's room.
Arthur was listening to his stereo
by candlelight.

"How can you listen to your stereo
with all the fuses blown?" said Father.
Arthur pointed to an extension cord
that went out the window.
The stereo was plugged into it.
"Where's the extension cord plugged in?"
said Father.

"Bill Boa's house," said Arthur.

Emma looked in. "I get the extension cord next," she said. "I'm watching the Wednesday Horror tonight."

"We'll talk about that after dinner," said Father.

"What dinner?" said Mother. "I've got sweet and sour spareribs in the oven but the oven won't go on."

"I'll put some fuses in," said Father.

"No fuses," said Arthur. "I gave Bill Boa our spare ones when he blew theirs today."

"Very clever," said Father. "Maybe you'd like to go over there and get ours back."

"You ever try to get anything back from a Boa?" said Arthur.

"All right then," said Father.
He unplugged Arthur's stereo and dragged
the extension cord into the kitchen.

"If you plug in the stove you'll blow
the Boas' fuses," said Mother.

"It's worth a try," said Father. "Anyhow
they're our fuses." He plugged in
the stove and turned on the oven.

"The Boas' house just went dark,"
said Emma, looking out of the window.

"We might as well eat out," said Father,
heading for the back door. "Let's go."

"There's Mr. Boa," said Arthur
as they drove off, "waving his end
of the extension cord at us."

"I'll explain to him later," said Father.

He drove to Hop Frog's Sun Luck
Chinese restaurant.

"I'm getting tired of Chinese food,"
said Emma. "This is the third time we've
eaten out this week, and it's all because
of Arthur and his Dracula Hi-Vamp."

"Oh, yes," said Arthur. "It's always me.
What about you? What were *you* doing
when the fuses blew?"

"What were you doing?"
said Father to Emma.

"Me?" said Emma. "I was ironing a blouse."

"While she was ironing, she was watching
the Early Horror on TV," said Arthur,
"plus wearing her Slimmo Electronic
Wonder-Massage belt and listening to
her stereo with headphones.
If you unplugged Emma, she wouldn't know
what to do."

"What about Mom?" said Emma. "She was
plugged into her bio-feedback machine,
listening to her alpha waves and watching

the yoga lady on the kitchen TV
and mixing kelp-and-carrot cocktails
in the blender."

"You see what I mean?" said Arthur.
"And everybody yells at me
for plugging in one little amplifier."

"Five hundred watts," said Mother.
"Or is it amps?"

DAVIS JOINT UNIFIED SCHOOLS
NORTH DAVIS ELEMENTARY

Just then the lights went out.
"I didn't do it," said Arthur.

"Power cut," said the waiter
when he brought a candle to the table.

"There," said Father.

16

"That's what happens when too many
people plug in too many things."

"Why did you *get* me a Dracula Hi-Vamp
if I can't plug it in?" said Arthur.

"How did I know we were going to wind up
living in darkness and eating out
every other night?" said Father.
"Arthur," he said, "have you ever
thought of playing a guitar that
doesn't use electricity?"

"What other kind is there?" said Arthur.
"Steam?"

"Don't get smart with me," said Father.
"I mean a plain one that just makes
whatever sound it makes."

"It wouldn't be the same," said Arthur.

"That's right," said Father. "It would be
different. It's time for some changes
around here."

When they got home, Father lit a candle
and went all around the house unplugging
things. He unplugged the electric
toothbrushes and his reducing machine
and his quadraphonic hi-fi. He unplugged
the bedroom TV and the kitchen TV
and the living-room TV. He unplugged
the blender and the bio-feedback
and the Slimmo. He unplugged Emma's
and Arthur's stereos, and he unplugged
the Dracula.

"What are you doing?" said Mother
and Emma and Arthur.

"Let's just give it a try," said Father.
"Let's see how long we can leave those
plugs unplugged."

"All right," said Mother. "We'll see
who's the first one to plug in."

19

When Father came home the next evening,
the lights were lit, but the house was
quiet. Mother was grinding kelp
and carrots by hand. She was wearing
her bio-feedback headphones. "They're not
plugged in," she said. "I just feel
more in touch with things this way."

Emma had a comic book propped up
against the TV. She was reading it
while she did her homework. She too was
wearing unplugged headphones.

"What are you listening to?" said Father.

"There's still a lot of sound left
in my head," said Emma, "and it feels
more natural this way."

"Where's Arthur?" said Father.

"Out," said Emma.

Father took his shoes off and sat down
in front of the TV. He looked at
his watch. "Please move the comic book,"
he said to Emma. "It's time for the news."

"The TV's not plugged in," said Emma.
"Remember?"

"I know," said Father, looking at
the dark screen. "But I don't want
to read a comic book while I'm thinking
about the news."

When Arthur came in Father said,
"How's it going without Dracula?"

"Quiet," said Arthur.

The next evening when Father came home,
Arthur was out again.
"It's so quiet here," said Father.

"You can listen to the frogs
and the crickets," said Mother.

"I am and it's driving me crazy,"
said Father. "How's the homework going?"
he said to Emma.

"She can't hear you," said Mother.
"She's wearing earplugs."

"Why is she wearing earplugs?"
said Father.

"The frogs and the crickets,"
said Mother.

"Maybe if we just plugged in *one* TV,"
said Father.

"If you watch the news, I watch
the Early Horror," said Emma.
"Fair's fair."

"I thought you couldn't hear me,"
said Father.

"I read your lips," said Emma.

Mother and Father and Emma were huddled
around the living-room TV
when Arthur came in.
"Who plugged in?" said Arthur.

"Three guesses," said Mother.

"After all," said Father, "we mustn't
cut ourselves off from the world.
You can play your stereo if you want to."

"That's all right," said Arthur.
"I have some reading to do."

"Reading?" said Father. "You?"

"All it takes is one light bulb,"
said Arthur.

Every day that week Arthur stayed
out of the house until dinnertime,
and after dinner he went out again.
Whenever Mother and Father and Emma
asked him what he was doing,
all he said was, "Saving power."

After two weeks Mother said to Father,
"It's starting to make me nervous to see
Arthur coming home with rosy cheeks
all the time. It isn't natural
for a crocodile to have rosy cheeks."

"It isn't just rosy cheeks," said Emma.
"He comes home with library books,
and he won't let me see them.
I'd like to know what he's up to."

"Arthur," said Father, "what *have* you
been doing all this time?"

"Show you Saturday," said Arthur.

On Saturday after lunch Arthur said,
"You want to see something?"
They all went into Arthur's room.
"Listen," said Arthur.
He plugged his guitar into the Dracula
Hi-Vamp and turned the amplifier on
and played the first few bars of *Suction.*

30

"Sounds like old times," said Father
to Mother.

"I can't hear you," said Mother.

"Look where it's plugged in," said Arthur.

The amplifier was plugged into
the extension cord and the extension cord
went out the window.

They went outside and followed it
down to the riverbank. The extension cord
was plugged into a wooden box.
Out of the box came a shaft,
and on the end of the shaft a waterwheel
was turning in the river.

"Water power," said Arthur. "Bill Boa
and I built the wheel and we made our own
generator out of secondhand parts."

"Arthur," said Mother,
"I'm so proud of you."

"Arthur," said Father,
"that's really something."

When they got back to the house,
Arthur turned up the volume
and settled down to play *Suction*
all the way through.
The windows rattled and the pictures
jumped up and down on the walls.
"That must be a pretty strong generator,"
said Father to Arthur. "I wonder
what kind of a picture we'd get
if we plugged the TV into it."

"Go ahead," said Arthur. "It's free."

Father plugged the living-room TV into
Arthur's extension cord.
"Look at that," he said. "What a picture."

"Crocodile power," said Emma,
and plugged in the Slimmo.

"I wonder if I still have any alpha waves,"
said Mother, and plugged in
the bio-feedback.

All of a sudden the music stopped,
the TV screen went dark,
and the Slimmo stopped vibrating.
"I can't hear any feedback
in my headphones," said Mother.

"We couldn't have blown the fuses
this time," said Emma.

"I think we blew Arthur's generator,"
said Father.

Emma looked into Arthur's room.
"Dracula's dead," she said,
"and Arthur's gone."

Mother and Father and Emma went
down to the river.

Arthur was sitting on the generator box
by the waterwheel.
He was playing his guitar by itself,
not plugged into anything.

"Sorry, Arthur," said Father.

"That's all right," said Arthur.
"I'm tired of all this machinery anyway."

"What's that you're playing?" said Mother.
"That's not *Suction,* is it?"

"No," said Arthur. "I'm making it up.
The wheel does the bass line,
and I just work in and out of it."

"It's very small and quiet," said Mother.

"Do you think it's too quiet?"
said Arthur.

"No," said Mother. "I think I could
get used to it. I really do."

"So could I," said Father.

"What are you going to call it?"
said Emma.

"Plugged-out Power," said Arthur.

ABOUT THE AUTHOR

Russell Hoban was born and brought up in Landsdale, Pennsylvania. He has written many distinguished and beloved books for children, including *Dinner at Alberta's, The Mouse and His Child, The Sorely Trying Day, The Little Brute Family,* and the very popular series of books about Frances the badger.

ABOUT THE ARTIST

The illustrator of a number of outstanding books for children, Byron Barton has also written and illustrated several books of his own, including *Hester; Buzz, Buzz, Buzz;* and *Jack and Fred.* Born in Pawtucket, Rhode Island, Mr. Barton now makes his home in New York City.